P9-BXZ-105

SEBGUGUGU THE GLUTTON

A Bantu Tale from Rwanda

Retold by
Verna Aardema

Illustrated by
Nancy L. Clouse

William B. Eerdmans Publishing Company
Grand Rapids, Michigan

Africa World Press
Trenton, New Jersey

SEBGUGUGU
THE
GLUTTON

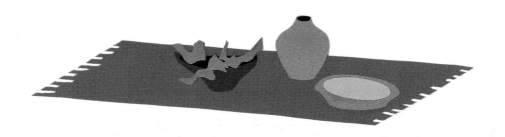

First published jointly 1993 by
Wm. B. Eerdmans Publishing Co.
255 Jefferson Ave. S.E., Grand Rapids, Michigan 49503
and Africa World Press, Inc.
15 Industry Court, Trenton, N.J. 08638

Printed in the United States of America

Library of Congress Cataloging-in-Publication Data

Aardema, Verna.
Sebgugugu the glutton: a Bantu tale from Rwanda /
retold by Verna Aardema; illustrated by Nancy L. Clouse.
p.   cm.
Summary: A greedy poor man tests the patience of Imana,
Lord of Rwanda, until he loses everything.
Eerdmans ISBN 0-8028-5073-1
Africa World Press ISBN 0-86543-377-1
1. Imana (Rundi deity) — Juvenile literature.   [1. Imana (Rundi deity)
2. Bantu speaking peoples — Folklore.   3. Folklore — Rwanda.]
I. Clouse, Nancy L., ill.   II. Title.
PZ8.1.A213Se   1993
[398.21] — dc20   92-44215
                                              CIP
                                              AC

Sebgugugu the Glutton, A Bantu Tale from Rwanda is a retelling of a story in Verna Aardema's book, *Behind the Back of the Mountain,* The Dial Press, 1973. That book is out-of-print and the rights have been returned to the author. The original source begins on page 45 in Alice Werner's *Myths and Legends of the Bantu,* George G. Harrap & Co., Ltd., London, 1933.

To Ryan Michael Adsit,
who is a glutton over Buszia's Paella
V.A.

Thanks to my mom and dad,
Margaret and Beryl Luttenton
N.C.

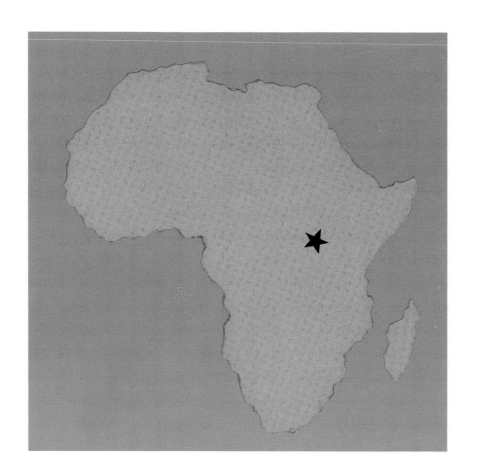

GLOSSARY AND GUIDE TO PRONUNCIATION

Amasi / A-MAH-see: Clotted milk, something like cottage cheese

Cattle kraal / Cattle krawl: A circular space enclosed by a thorn fence

Gitale / Gee-TAH-lay: The cow

Igwababa / Ee-GWA-ba-ba: The crow

Imana / Ee-MAH-na: Lord of Rwanda

KWICH / KWEECH

LOOO!: An exclamation

Marula plum / Mah-ROO-la: The wild plum of Southern Africa

Mealie porridge / MEE-lee porridge: Cornmeal mush

Rwanda / Roo-AHN-da: A small country east of Zaire

Sebgugugu / Seb-GOO-goo-goo

T'CHI / T'CHEE

Unanana / You-NAH-na-na

Zabala / Za-BAH-la

Zitu / Zee-too

Sebgugugu was a poor man. All he owned in this world was a cow named Gitale. One day while Unanana, his wife, was out hoeing in her garden in the forest, Sebgugugu sat in front of his hut.

As he rested, a little bird alighted, *ta,* on a nearby shrub and began to sing:

> Guli-gu, guli-gu
> Kalli-kah, kalli-kah,
> Kah, kah, kah, kaah.

As Sebgugugu listened, it seemed to him that the bird was singing words that he could understand. He thought it was saying:

> "Sebgugugu, Sebgugugu,
> Kill the cow, kill the cow,
> And get a hundred."

At the end of the day, when Unanana returned with their baby, Zitu, and their little boy, Zabala, the bird came again and sang:

Guli-gu, guli-gu,
Kalli-kah, kalli-kah,
Kah, kah, kah, kaah.

Sebgugugu said, "Listen, Unanana. Do you hear what that bird is saying?"

"Saying!" cried Unanana. "It is only singing."

Sebgugugu said, "It is saying, 'Sebgugugu, kill the cow and get a hundred.'"

"Nonsense!" cried Unanana. "You are just hungry for meat."

"No," said Sebgugugu. "I think Imana is sending us a message through that bird."

Unanana listened again as the bird sang. But she could hear no words. She said, "Sebgugugu, we have to feed our children on Gitale's milk. If you kill her, they will starve! Please, don't do anything so foolish!"

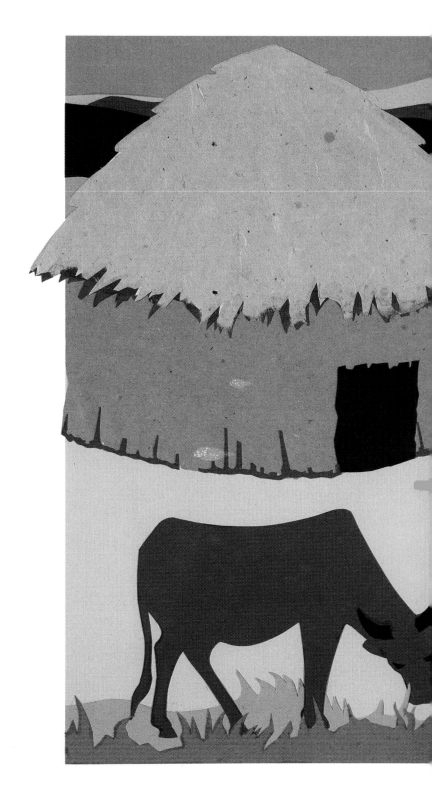

But Sebgugugu never listened to his wife. The very next day, he killed the cow. And not one cow appeared in her place.

The family ate meat for many days. But when the meat was gone, they all became very hungry. So Sebgugugu put Zitu into a basket, which Unanana carried on her head. Then he took Zabala by the hand, and they set out in search of food.

The family walked a long way without finding anything at all. At last they sat down by the path to rest.

Then Sebgugugu cried out, "Oh, Imana, Lord of Rwanda, what shall we do?"

Imana heard, and he suddenly appeared before them. He led them to a wonderful vine with all kinds of fruits and vegetables growing on it. He said, "You may pluck the fruit, but do not harm the vine."

For many days the family lived off the bounty of that vine. Then one day Sebgugugu said, "Unanana, that plant would produce more if I trimmed it."

"Oh, Sebgugugu," cried Unanana, "remember what Imana said! Don't do anything so foolish!"

But Sebgugugu never listened to his wife. And, *tch, tch, tch,* he began chopping off the sprawling branches. Soon, the vine withered and died.

Again the family was without food.

And again, Sebgugugu prayed to Imana for help. This time the Creator led them to a great rock with a crack in it. At a word from Imana, food came bubbling out of the opening, *gu-bu-du*. Amasi, mealie porridge, and honey! Imana said, "You may take the food, but do not disturb the rock."

For many days the family lived off that food. But it came forth slowly. It took a long time to fill a basket. And one day Sebgugugu said, "The crack is too narrow. I'm going to make it wider."

Unanana cried, "Oh, Sebgugugu, don't do anything so foolish!"

But Sebgugugu never listened to his wife. He sharpened one end of a big pole and hardened the tip of it in the fire. Then he thrust the point into the crack and pried, KWICH!

Imana saw him do that. And he caused the crack to close completely.

Again the family was without food. Once more they set out in search of it. They walked a long way without finding so much as a marula plum. Then Sebgugugu cried out, "Oh, Imana, Lord of Rwanda, help us or we will die!"

Imana heard, and he appeared before them. He pointed to a distant hill and said, "Beyond that hill is a cattle kraal. Go there and live on the milk from the cows. They are cared for by Igwababa the crow. You must give him some of the milk. And never be unkind to him or harm him, for he is my faithful servant."

Sebgugugu and his family hurried on.

Beyond the hill they found the cattle kraal. There was no one there, but they found vessels full of milk. When Sebgugugu had drunk all he wanted, he gave his wife some, and she fed the children. Then they all sat down and waited to see what would happen.

When the sun was low, they saw the cattle coming. No herd boys ran beside them. But a white-necked crow kept flying to and fro above them, calling GWE, GWE, GWE. In that way, it drove the cows into the cattlefold.

Sebgugugu and his household lived near that cattle kraal for several years. But finally, Sebgugugu became restless.

One day he said, "Unanana, our children are big enough to herd cattle. I don't see what we want with that old crow! I shall kill him, and then all the cows will belong to us."

"Oh, Sebgugugu," begged Unanana, "please don't do anything so foolish!"

But Sebgugugu never listened to his wife. That evening he went out with his bow and arrow and lay in wait for the crow.

When Igwababa came driving the cattle through the gate, Sebgugugu let the arrow fly, T'CHI!

The bird came down in a flurry of black feathers.

Then, LOOO! Imana's patience was at an end. He caused the cattle, and even Unanana and the children, to disappear without leaving a trace.

Sebgugugu, because of his greed and disobedience, had lost all that he had.

The End

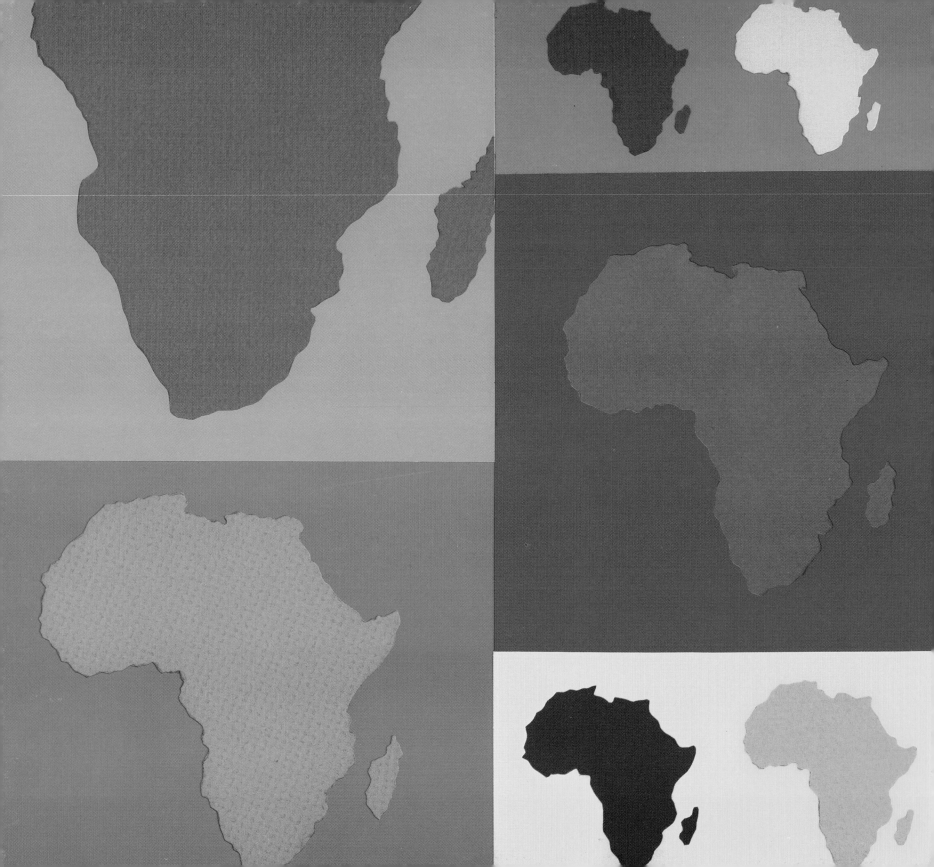